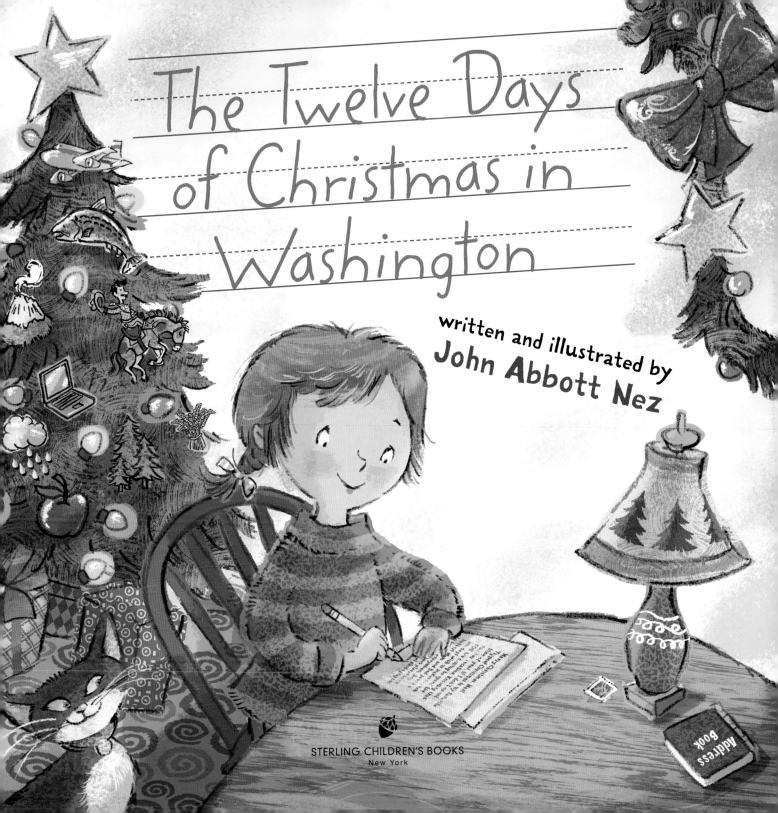

The Twelve Days of Christmas in Washington

written and illustrated by
John Abbott Nez

STERLING CHILDREN'S BOOKS
New York

Merry Christmas, Max!

Yippee! Christmas is my favorite time of year, if I don't count summer vacation. Knowing that YOU are coming to spend the holidays with us makes it even better!

Mom and Dad promise to take us everywhere. Dad knows all the best places to go since he's a travel photographer. From our houseboat on Puget Sound, we'll be seeing lots of boats and water, so be sure to bring your sea legs.

Have you ever seen fish that fly? Or a pod of orca whales? Me neither, but I want to! We'll go looking for lumberjacks and cowboys, volcanoes and totem poles. Who knows, we might even see Bigfoot! And don't worry, Mount St. Helens probably won't blow its top while you're here.

Washington's called the "Evergreen State" because we've got more evergreens than the biggest Christmas tree farm you can imagine!

We'll be at the airport to meet your plane!

Molly

Dear Mom & Dad,

Wow, what a flight! Our jet zoomed right past Mount Rainier as we came in to land in Seattle. The pilot said it's the tallest mountain in Washington. Mount Rainier is a giant volcano . . . a dormant one, luckily. That means it's asleep and won't erupt anytime soon (fingers crossed).

From the plane I got a really close look at the mountains. Molly was right about Washington being the "Evergreen State." I've never seen so many trees!

Molly, Uncle George, and Aunt Martha were all hugs at the airport when they picked me up. As a gift, Molly gave me a little willow goldfinch. Molly's already named him Hopalong. I call him Hoppy for short. He hops and flutters along with us everywhere we go. I also got a western hemlock seedling in a cup. Molly's the best gift giver ever! Now I have the official state bird and tree.

Love,
Max

All hands on deck!

We sailed away today on a ferryboat! Aunt Martha drove us down a ramp into the ferry docked in Seattle where cars were packed in like sardines. We walked up on deck to see the view, and I nearly jumped a foot when a GINORMOUS loud toot blasted from the boat's horn! A passing ferry gave out a big toot, too.

Our boat sailed across Puget Sound to the Olympic Peninsula. We saw freighters from China, tugboats, giant cruise ships, and sailboats. With the salty sea air blowing and the ferry rolling up and down, it was easy to pretend to be a pirate sailing the high seas. Noisy gulls circled all around hoping for food.

After the ferry docked on Bainbridge Island we drove through a thick, deep rainforest where everything was green and covered with ferns and moss. Just now we're heading to an historic seaport called Port Townsend, where we'll stay overnight. Molly says there are supposed to be ghosts there since it's so old!

Ahoy, matey!
Max

On the second day of Christmas,
my cousin gave to me . . .

2 ferryboats

and a goldfinch in a hemlock tree.

Shiver Me Timbers!

Lucky for us we survived the night ghost-free, and there was no time to think about ghosts this morning—we went whale watching! The sign on the pier read: "See the Orcas and Marine Mammals of Puget Sound." So our happy-go-lucky crew walked the plank to step aboard the <u>Smiling Tides</u>.

Captain Pete, the boat's skipper, told us that orcas live together in family groups called pods. They hunt and swim together, just like a family. We soon spied some seals and harbor porpoises, but they jumped too fast for good pictures. Finally we got lucky and spotted a pod of whales near the San Juan Islands!

The skipper brought the boat to a stop for a closer look. The orcas blew big clouds of water vapor when they came up for air.

Captain Pete said that orcas are also known as "Killer Whales." They might have a scary name, but don't worry, Mom, they don't eat people—they only eat fish and seals.

Thar she blows!
Max

On the third day of Christmas,
my cousin gave to me . . .

Smiling Tides

3 huge whales

2 ferryboats,
and a goldfinch in a hemlock tree.

Yodelayheehoo!

I think that's how alpine yodelers say "It's beautiful in the mountains!" All day Molly and I jingled sleigh bells and tooted giant alpenhorns in the snowy town of Leavenworth. This town looks just like an alpine village tucked inside a snow globe. Molly and I ate a whole lot goat cheese and tried slap dancing with lederhosen. (It's a whole lot harder than it looks!) We even went on a sleigh ride through the woods. Molly made me play a bell in the handbell ringers program. The song was pretty easy, so I didn't goof up too much.

Tonight we listened to an alpine choir in top hats and red shawls AND we watched the lighting of the Christmas lights. It was all very "gemütliche und wunderbar." (That means it was "cozy and wonderful" in German.)

We even gave yodeling a try. Hoppy's feathers were a little ruffled by all the jangling sleigh bells and blasting alpenhorns!

Your yodeling son,
Max

On the fourth day of Christmas,
my cousin gave to me . . .

4 alpenhorns

3 huge whales, 2 ferryboats,
and a goldfinch in a hemlock tree.

Look out for flying fish!

Today we went holiday shopping at Pike Place Market in Seattle. The fish sellers there have a tradition of tossing fish high over the counter. I ducked as trout went zooming over my head. This waterfront market is over 100 years old, but it was all new to me.

We saw farmers unloading pickup trucks and tried amazing new foods. Molly talked me into trying piroshky, which is a pastry bun stuffed with spinach, cheese, and onions. Yum! Who knew spinach could be so tasty?

Jugglers and street musicians entertained the crowd. I tried joining the street band for fun, with spoons and a washboard. Hopalong tweeted, too.

Aunt Martha bought bouquets of flowers. Then we shopped at artists' stalls filled with hand-woven sweaters and hand-blown glass. (There was even a tattoo shop, but don't worry, Dad, I didn't get one.)

I'm going to have to practice juggling and trout tossing for my next visit.

We fish you a Merry Christmas!

Max

On the fifth day of Christmas,
my cousin gave to me . . .

5 golden trout

4 alpenhorns, 3 huge whales, 2 ferryboats,
and a goldfinch in a hemlock tree.

Mush those huskies!

Wow! They sure do have some BIG trees up here in Washington. Some as tall as a 38-story building! A whole class of kids holding hands could barely reach around the trunk of one of these cedar trees. Today we mushed by dogsled up to Mount Rainier National Park. Talk about fun!

Aunt Martha explained that the old growth trees we saw along the trail might live 1,000 years to become the giants of the forest. I'd guess Bigfoot would have an easy time hiding out in these woods. Bigfoot is a mythical creature who is <u>very</u> popular around here. No one's ever captured one, but people keep trying. We spotted some suspiciously LARGE footprints in the snow . . . could Bigfoot have passed right by us??

The rainforests of the Pacific Northwest are GREAT for growing trees. With all these trees, it's easy to see why loggers and wood carving are part of the history of Washington.

Timber!
Max

On the sixth day of Christmas,
my cousin gave to me . . .

6 giant footprints

5 golden trout, 4 alpenhorns,
3 huge whales, 2 ferryboats,
and a goldfinch in a hemlock tree.

Yo! Mom & Dad,

Molly and I were groovin' in the Jet City today. Seattle is nicknamed the Jet City because they build so many jet airplanes here.

You'll never guess how we got around town. Nope, not on a plane, and not on a boat this time . . . on a monorail! That's a space-age train that zips on a rail high above the traffic.

Aunt Martha took us to the Space Needle for lunch. It's the most famous building in Seattle. I got a little dizzy when the glass elevator zoomed us up to the top. The Space Needle and the monorail were both built for the Seattle World's Fair of 1962.

After lunch we went to the Experience Music Project/Science Fiction Museum. It's a wild-looking museum about popular culture, filled with exhibits about music (and aliens, too). Molly told me that grunge music and Jimi Hendrix both came from Seattle. I even got to see Jimi's guitar!

The Seattle Public Library was our next stop—I don't think I've ever been in a cooler library. It's like a crazy greenhouse put together from giant puzzle pieces.

Movin' and groovin',
Max

Hi, Mom & Dad,

I wonder how walruses and wolves might celebrate Christmas in Washington? Maybe with bells on their whiskers and wagging wolf tails? Or maybe they get their chuckles from the laughing kookaburra. That bird sure made Molly and me laugh.

At the Point Defiance Zoo & Aquarium in Tacoma, Molly and I got to visit a zoo and an aquarium at the same time! We saw polar bears, musk oxen, and Pacific walruses. They looked right at home in this cold winter weather.

I got some great snapshots of exotic land animals and cool sea creatures, too. They also have a collection of exotic bugs. (Molly was glad most of those were behind glass. She doesn't like bugs.)

We had lunch at the nearby Museum of Glass on the waterfront. We got to walk across the amazing Bridge of Glass. I took pictures of some shining glass sculptures. This artwork hangs from the ceiling and looks just like some of the giant sea creatures we saw at the aquarium—all wavy and squishy and glowing with magic.

Having a wild good time!

Max

On the eighth day of Christmas,
my cousin gave to me . . .

8 wild
wonders

7 jets a-zooming, 6 giant footprints, 5 golden trout,
4 alpenhorns, 3 huge whales, 2 ferryboats,
and a goldfinch in a hemlock tree.

Howdy, Buckaroos!

Molly and I sang cowboy songs as the car rolled along the highway. A billboard sign read: Howdy! Welcome to Washington's Cowboy Country! The scenery here is high and dry, almost like a desert. We were heading for Dusty's Rambling Ranch, where Molly and I got to ride horses! It was a little scary at first, but my horse, Billy-Bud, soon made me feel like a pal. (Especially after I fed him a few apples.)

Uncle George explained that in the summer Ellensburg and Omak have big rodeos with bucking broncos and steer roping. They also hold Pow-Wows. That's when Native Americans get together for a big celebration. Molly says the dancing, food, and storytelling at the Pow-Wows are amazing.

Meanwhile, back on the ranch, Aunt Martha schooled us on cowboy lingo. I've learned about roundups, stampedes, and wranglers. I might even write a little cowboy poetry. What rhymes with "jingling spurs"?

Happy Trails!
Max

Hi, Mom & Dad,

Ugh! I was already saddle sore from yesterday's ride, but tonight I also have a bellyache. I think I just ate too much apple pie after dinner.

Today we toured the orchards and vineyards of central Washington. We stopped at a country store near Wenatchee. The menu explained that Washington grows more apples than any other state . . . also more hops, red raspberries, and sweet cherries. Add in some pear trees and I'd guess this is about the tastiest part of Washington! I've never seen so much fruit in one place!

Aunt Martha said that this part of the state is called the "dry side." Here the weather is sunny and dry—just perfect for locally grown fruit.

In the late afternoon, Molly and I wandered all over a snowy apple orchard. We worked up quite an appetite, so I guess that's why I ate so much pie after dinner. Or maybe it just tasted too good to resist!

Sorely yours,
Max

On the tenth day of Christmas,
my cousin gave to me . . .

10 apples gleaming

9 cowboys crooning, 8 wild wonders,
7 jets a-zooming, 6 giant footprints, 5 golden trout,
4 alpenhorns, 3 huge whales, 2 ferryboats,
and a goldfinch in a hemlock tree.

Ho! Ho! Ho!

Today we drove along the Columbia River, the largest river in Washington. Woody Guthrie, a folk singer, wrote a song about it called, "Roll On Columbia, Roll On." It's the official state folk song.

In Spokane, Molly and I went snow shoeing in Riverfront Park. The snowdrifts were <u>super</u> deep. We saw the world's biggest red wagon—a <u>giant</u> sculpture 12 feet high and 27 feet long. It can hold as many as 300 people! Molly and I discovered another sculpture of a garbage-eating goat. We fed it some candy wrappers . . . because you're supposed to feed it litter to keep the park clean. Hopalong even cleaned up a gum wrapper.

Downtown, the stores were playing songs by Bing Crosby, who grew up in Spokane. He was a movie star and a singer, too. His most famous song is probably "White Christmas." I guess it must be a classic if even <u>I've</u> heard it.

Dreaming of a white Christmas,
Max

On the eleventh day of Christmas, my cousin gave to me . . .

11 skiers swooshing

10 apples gleaming, **9** cowboys crooning, **8** wild wonders,
7 jets a-zooming, **6** giant footprints, **5** golden trout,
4 alpenhorns, **3** huge whales, **2** ferryboats,
and a goldfinch in a hemlock tree.

Deck the Halls, Mom & Dad!

Today we drove back from Spokane to Seattle to visit the Center for Wooden Boats. People come here to learn to build and sail wooden boats. I'll put "boat building" on my wish list for next time I visit.

At sunset, Molly and I roasted marshmallows on a bonfire and watched Christmas ships sailing on Lake Union. In the holiday season, people gather around bonfires to sing carols and keep warm. The crackling fire and sweet carols got me feeling all Christmassy. And it snowed! I think I was a little misty-eyed from it all . . . or maybe it was just the smoke from the marshmallows I kept accidentally setting on fire.

Molly has invited us all to come back to visit this summer! But tomorrow I'll be flying back home on a big shining jet built right here in Washington. Be sure to bring a truck to the airport to pick up all the stuff I'm bringing back!

Already making my list for next summer,
Max

On the twelfth day of Christmas,
my cousin gave to me . . .

12 boats a-blinking

11 skiers swooshing, 10 apples gleaming, 9 cowboys crooning,
8 wild wonders, 7 jets a-zooming, 6 giant footprints,
5 golden trout, 4 alpenhorns, 3 huge whales, 2 ferryboats,
and a goldfinch in a hemlock tree.

Washington: The Evergreen State

Capital: Olympia • **State abbreviation:** WA • **Largest city:** Seattle • **State flower:** the coast rhododendron
State fossil: Columbian mammoth • **State bird:** the willow goldfinch • **State marine mammal:** the orca • **State tree:** the western hemlock • **State fruit:** the apple • **State motto:** *Al-ki*—a Chinook word meaning "by and by"

Some Famous Washingtonians:

William O. Douglas (1898–1980) grew up in Yakima and attended Whitman College in Walla Walla. His tenure as a Supreme Court justice lasted for nearly 37 years—the longest in U.S. history. Nicknamed "Wild Bill," he became best known for his outspoken opinions in favor of unfettered free speech, environmental issues, and upholding the rights of the accused.

Mary Davenport Engberg (1880–1951) was born in a covered wagon near Spokane. After showing an early interest in music, she mastered the violin, and performed throughout Europe. She gave her first solo performance with the Seattle Symphony in 1908, and went on to organize the Davenport Engberg Orchestra in Bellingham. She led its opening concert in 1914, becoming the first female orchestra conductor in the U.S.

Thea Christiansen Foss (aka **Tugboat Annie**) (1857–1927) founded the Foss Maritime Company in Tacoma in 1889. She began by renting out a single rowboat, and her business grew to the point that she ran a whole fleet of ships. Her life story was later turned into a Hollywood movie called *Tugboat Annie.*

Fay Fuller (1869–1958), a journalist and schoolteacher living in Yelm, was the first woman known to reach the summit of Mount Rainier. This was an extraordinary achievement for a woman in 1890, and Fuller attracted much criticism. Her climbing gear, which included flannel bloomers, was considered very immodest. Undaunted by her critics, Fuller was successful in her efforts to spur interest in mountain climbing in the Pacific Northwest. Fay Peak, about six miles from Mount Rainier, is named in her honor.

Betty MacDonald (1908–1958) was an author of humorous books such as the Mrs. Piggle-Wiggle series. She lived in Seattle and on a farm on Vashon Island. Her very funny book *The Egg and I* recounted her adventures on a chicken farm near Port Townsend.

Francis Richard "Dick" Scobee (1939–1986) was born in Cle Elum. Selected for NASA's astronaut program, he successfully piloted a mission into space in 1984. Tragically, he was killed while commanding the Space Shuttle *Challenger* in 1986. After Scobee's death, he was awarded the Purple Heart medal, the Congressional Space Medal of Honor, and was inducted into the Astronaut Hall of Fame.

Mount St. Helens (erupted 1980)

On May 18, 1980, Mount St. Helens, located 96 miles south of Seattle, blew its top. It was the biggest volcanic event in the history of the United States. For months, the mountain had been awakening with steam venting and earthquakes. Then a giant bulge formed in the side of the volcano, a sign that magma was rising from deep beneath the Earth's surface. Finally, the mountain erupted at 8:32 a.m. with a cataclysmic explosion.

The huge mushroom cloud of ash grew to a height of 12 miles and spread into the stratosphere for 10 hours, spewing ash for hundreds of miles downwind. Cars were buried in ash, roofs were coated, and people living in the area choked on dust.

The eruption reduced the height of Mount St. Helens by 1,300 feet, leaving behind a crater one mile wide.

Tragically, 57 people were killed, 250 homes were destroyed, and 47 bridges disappeared beneath the volcanic debris. It left behind a massive trail of destruction throughout the entire region. Scientists (who are getting better and better at warning people of impending disasters) predict that the volcanoes of Washington are likely to erupt again one day, since the Cascade Mountains are part of the Pacific "Ring of Fire."

To Ann, Arthur, and Evan . . . who have always lived in Washington. Thanks for all the great times we've had exploring the natural wonders of the Evergreen State.

STERLING CHILDREN'S BOOKS
New York

An Imprint of Sterling Publishing
387 Park Avenue South
New York, NY 10016

STERLING CHILDREN'S BOOKS and the distinctive Sterling Children's Books logo
are trademarks of Sterling Publishing Co., Inc.

Text and illustrations © 2011 by John Abbott Nez

ISBN 978-1-4027-7068-5 (Hardcover)

Distributed in Canada by Sterling Publishing
c/o Canadian Manda Group, 165 Dufferin Street
Toronto, Ontario, Canada M6K 3H6
Distributed in the United Kingdom by GMC Distribution Services
Castle Place, 166 High Street, Lewes, East Sussex, England BN7 1XU
Distributed in Australia by Capricorn Link (Australia) Pty. Ltd.
P.O. Box 704, Windsor, NSW 2756, Australia

The original illustrations for this book were created in multiple media
(pencils, pens, brushes, watercolors, and Adobe Photoshop)

For information about custom editions, special sales, and premium and corporate purchases,
please contact Sterling Special Sales at 800-805-5489 or specialsales@sterlingpublishing.com.

Printed in China
Lot #:
6 8 10 9 7
05/17
www.sterlingpublishing.com/kids

CANADA

Washington

Montana

Oregon

Idaho

Wyoming

Nevada

Utah

Colorado

California

Arizona

New Mexico

Hawaii

Alaska

(NOT TO SCALE)

MEXICO